Missing Traits of an Unseen Goddess

Darrell Dwayne Bernard Mallard II

ISBN 978-1-63784-739-8 (paperback)
ISBN 978-1-63784-740-4 (digital)

Hawes & Jenkins Publishing
16427 N Scottsdale Road Suite 410
Scottsdale, AZ 85254
www.hawesjenkins.com

Printed in the United States of America

The suicide rate of young Americans has increased drastically. Studies link these self-inflicted deaths to most mental illnesses and depression. When we as individuals consider ourselves worthless and less valued than our peers, this creates an emotional disturbance that interferes with our ability to make rational decisions. Everyone wants to be noticed. We as humans have an insatiable need for attention. When this attention is not received, our frustration only builds and causes us to dislike ourselves. When we dislike ourselves, this will more than often lead to drug use, and association among the wrong crowd to fulfill our need to be accepted and recognized. Deadly school shootings, and other acts of attention seeking behavior has not come from children who were mentally ill. When we are rejected and grow to feel neglected, this hatred of ourselves and those who fail to acknowledge us will only force most to find a way to inflict the same pain they have suffered. This is what has led many to take their own lives, and the lives of their peers. This is something you can control. When we find ourselves, and love who we are, no longer will we seek validation and devalue the worth of our being when we don't receive recognition from those who are without value.

1

The conduct and moralistic values of a goddess rises above the common standards of the average woman. Beautiful both inside and out, the inner beauty that radiates from her soul releases a glow that brings light to all things in her presence. There is nothing that shines brighter. You are your worth. The worth and value of a goddess is reflected by a true and unconditional love for self. A goddess is the treasure of a god. In the eyes of a god, nothing is more valuable.

Since the fourth grade Katesha and Jeremy had a crush on one another. Throughout their years together in middle school, the two had been in love. Much had not changed since then. As far as she knew, Jeremy still loved her, but lately during the end of their sophomore year the way things had taken a turn Katesha didn't know how much longer their relationship would last.

For more than two weeks she had begun to be overrun by more news on social media about how her boyfriend had started to date another girl. Things like this had never happened in the past. Her instinct told her that these stories could not have all been made up. No one would be as desperate to claim that they were in a relationship with anyone who had not been leading them on. She had asked Jeremy to be honest, though while he had only denied the rumors, she had no proof to believe she had been lied to.

On this Friday morning, only minutes after she had been awakened for school, before she could brush her teeth, Katesha heard a buzzing from her phone as she received and read a message from her best friend advising her to check her Snapchat.

Unique

Girl, check your snap. ASAP!!! 5:35 AM

Logging onto Snapchat where in addition to all of those who had begun to taunt her by claiming that she had been a "Nobody", and wasn't worth being with someone like Jeremy, there had been a screenshot on FaceBook from a shared post made by Amelia on Instagram.

Amelia had been the captain of the varsity cheerleading squad and the school's track star. Tall, athletic with full and well-developed body parts, Amelia was ranked as the most beautiful and popular girl in the school.

Most would consider Katesha lame. Since the beginning of her school years, she had been an honor student. Katesha had been awarded scholarships from several colleges and knew that once she graduated and earned a degree, her aunt would be proud that she had not wasted time going to school simply to earn a general diploma that would only qualify her for employment at a fast-food restaurant or department store. Most young women were satisfied with low paying minimum wage jobs. Most lacked vision and did not have the drive and determination to put forth the needed effort to become great. Her aunt understood this. Values can't be taught by anyone who is worthless with low value. You can only become like the women or woman who has the most influence in your life. She had always wanted more for her niece and for this reason her aunt continued to instruct and guide her by being the virtuous women she wanted her to be.

She had been smart, and her intellect had been noticed by most who worked for, and attended the school, though compared to Amelia, she considered herself to be a loser. Girls who were well-known and liked didn't gravitate and follow her everywhere she went. Some days she believed she was pretty, only when she was told so. She didn't have thousands of followers or friends who followed her on social media. She only had her best friend, and to everyone else who Unique may as well have been a ghost, she had also been considered a loser and among the "Nobodies".

Overwhelmed with emotion as the thought of the girl being everything, she believed she could never be to Jeremy, Katesha then logged off social media.

Calling Jeremy's cellular phone, what had first gone to the voicemail, though as Katesha called back for the third time, the phone was answered not by Jeremy, but a voice she had heard many times during prep rallies, morning announcements, and all other events the school had used Amelia to promote and draw a crowd.

"Who is this?" Katesha asked, clearly aware of who the girl had been.

Hearing laughter from the background as Amelia giggled, she said, "Someone you are not.

Haven't you heard about us? Jeremy no longer wants to be with you. I'm his new girlfriend Katesha."

After Amelia had hung up, and Katesha had called back for the fifth time, the girl had finally answered the phone again.

"What part of that didn't you understand?" Amelia snapped before Katesha could say anything.

Choking over her words as her voice became hoarse as the tears began to roll down her face, Katesha said, "No, let Jeremy tell me that for himself."

"He doesn't want to talk. Everything you need to know has already been said, so bye Katesha."

Staring aimlessly at the screen of her phone, where there had still been a picture of her and Jeremy, it did not take long to figure out what she would do.

After her mother and father had died while she had still been in elementary, Jeremy had been the only person and thing she had to live for. He had been everything and the bond they shared was the only thing that mattered. If they were no longer together, and he was with someone else, then there was no reason for her to live, or to allow them to live and be happy together.

On any other day you would not have seen Katesha walking down 12th Court. From the school the street had been the short cut to her house, but with her aunt being a devoted Christian who believed that the Lord Jesus Christ would fight all their battles, there was no other place she knew to find a gun.

Paranoid as if the police would drive up and arrest her at any moment, for not only the murders she had yet to commit but being that she was near a well-known drug house, she knew that if not any other place in her neighborhood this was one place she was not supposed to be.

Stepping into the yard, where she started pass the driveway and approached the two-story building, a black SUV pulled in fast behind her. Stopping in her tracks as she then tried to look through the dark tint, only to be met by a vague reflection of her own image, only moments later the boy had exited the vehicle and began to study Katesha as if the girl had been a strange and unfamiliar creature.

During the time the two had gone to school together he had continuously pursued her, though throughout all those years he had never been given a chance. There were many girls who had done outrageous and unimaginable things to get his attention, but out of all the girls he had known, Katesha had been the last one he ever expected to show up at his trap.

Wearing a black turban, what most of the boys from the neighborhood who could be seen around him often wore, Darrell said, "What are you doing around here?"

Aware that he had only ever known her to be a good house girl, who had probably never gotten into any trouble, Katesha said, "I need to talk to you."

"Talk to me about what?" He asked appearing to check the time on his wrist while taking a step forward before turning back.

"When I wanted to talk to you, you didn't want to give me no play and acted like you was too good for me."

Focusing her attention on the sound of both the front and back passenger side doors closing as one of the boys who held an assault rifle crossed in front of the vehicle before another then exited and followed the two, Katesha said, "No this is serious, and I have never thought I was too good for you. It was because I already had a boyfriend, and that is the reason I'm here to talk to you now."

Smirking as he silenced the phone that buzzed in his hand, Darrell said, "So what you saying you want to be with me?"

"No. I need a gun. That is who I am going to use it on. I am going to kill him and his new girlfriend."

"You are tripping." Darrell said scanning the street as if the girl had really come to set him up and had been working undercover for the police or someone who wanted him dead.

"I'm not about to give you a gun, so what after you catch a body you tell the law that you got the gun from me, and then I get charged with conspiracy to commit murder?"

"I'm not going to get caught or go to jail." Katesha stated assuring that she had a plan.

"After I kill them, and all of her friends who posted comments about me, I'm going to save one bullet for myself."

Taking the girl for a ride, where only moments after they had got inside the SUV and driven away, they watched as three unmarked police vehicles passed turning on their lights and blocked an old Nissan Altima with dark tints before exiting and approaching the vehicle with their guns drawn.

Using the touch sensitive controls to check the surround view camera. With the provided features of the new Cayenne, the device had been reprogrammed, which allowed its radar system to detect and show whether either of the officers had begun to follow him. Readjusting the format, as he then apologized to the girl for the disturbance, Darrell said, "Now break everything down and tell me what happened."

Listening intently while maintaining as much possible eye contact, which had then been when he noticed that the girl had truly been deranged, and had neglected all intentions of fixing or doing anything to her hair, Katesha said, "So you haven't seen what everybody has been saying about me?"

"Saying about you where?"

"On social media."

Shaking his head, Darrell said, "I have never been on there. I might have caught a few clips when I have been shown things, but I'm not really a social media ass nigga. There is too much goofy shit that distracts niggas and take your mind away from reality and what you should be focused on."

Thinking of the few times he had been shown videos of girls dancing on TikTok, and how each girl repeated the same dances and appeared to have the same perception as most young women he spoke to who were lost with nothing more in their head and to offer anyone except an urge to show their bodies, what most believed had been all they needed to attract and keep the attention of a man who would possibly notice them and change their life, Darrell said, "Anything that doesn't put money in my pockets, I don't entertain it."

Staring quizzically at the boy being that even though she had never known of him to have a page, not that she had ever searched, but with many people speaking about him, on both social media and throughout their neighborhood, she had assumed that he would be one in the know of anything that had been happening among the "in" crowd.

"Well…" Katesha said.

"First off you know me and Jeremy have been together since…, well before you ever tried to talk to me. Everything has been so good, but now he has left me to be with Amelia, and now everybody from Dillard has been posting comments and laughing at me."

"What Amelia are you talking about?" Darrell asked unsure, though unmistakably believing the girl had been referring to the same Amelia that he had once had sex with before allowing six of his friends to exchange intercourse with her.

"I'm talking about Amelia Lockhart."

Crossing Sistrunk Boulevard as they proceeded further down 27th Avenue, Darrell said, "I don't know what would make him choose someone like her over you, but before I take you back to the hood, I want to show you something."

Entering Boulevard Gardens, a neighborhood better known as Tater Town, where the boy had drove before stopping at a house that had been located directly behind a cemetery.

Exiting the SUV, Darrell said, "Get out. This is my auntie house. Just follow me."

Opening the side gate that led to the women's backyard, where the two then made their way to the fence that crossed over to the cemetery, Darrell said, "Do you know how to jump fences?"

"Jump the fence for what? I don't want to go over there."

Being that at 6:25 A.M the sun had yet to rise, Katesha said, "I'm not going inside no graveyard, especially while its dark."

Looking the girl in her eyes as he took her hand to lead her toward the fence, Darrell, said, "Trust me. I won't let anything happen to you I promise."

Walking through the cemetery where they passed between lots and down a dark road that led to the other end, Katesha had begun to hold tightly onto him as she tiptoed and jumped as if whenever she had made the mistake of walking over someone's grave, she had been stepping on the dead person's body.

Standing over a head stone that had been next to a disturbed patch of grass where someone had recently been buried, and had yet to be given a marker as Darrell then pointed at the ground, he said, "Do you see the name on there?"

Looking up at the boy as she read the familiar name of one of their former classmates, he said, "I was supposed to died long time ago. That day that happened to him, the other boy who they said was with him, who they said they couldn't find and thought died in that house, that was me.

"Do you believe in spirits? What if I told you that I was something else that people wouldn't understand, and that I was still here for a reason?"

Tensing as she clutched tighter to the boy who she had wanted to run away from as he had begun to send chills through her body, Darrell said, "Everybody is in this world for a purpose. If you kill yourself then what will you gain? You will only lose that opportunity to prove that you are something greater than what people believe you are.

"You say that people have been picking on you, but tell me what does their opinion matter? If you kill yourself because of them then you are defeated, but to continue, you will defeat them through the strength of your mind.

"There are a lot of people who like to run from their problems. They use drugs, not only because they think that it will impress those who they are seeking recognition from, but they believe that it will allow them to escape their problems. The truth is that by using any drug it will only make the situation worse. You must deal with the real issue which lies within yourself.

"What do you think the soul is?"

Taking in the scenery as the thought of spirits made her think of herself being dead and trapped alone inside of a box underneath the ground, Darrell said, "The soul is who you are and will always be. Our soul never dies. When you run from your fears and don't face them, your spirit and the soul that is inside of you holds that fear.

"You will never be free until you conquer your fears. If you kill yourself, you will only curse your soul and deal with those same fears until you face them. Using drugs is the same as putting a gun to your head. When you come down from your high, the problems you are trying to escape will still be there.

"No matter what you are going through your life is not over. Jeremy is not the only one who could make you happy, and for him to leave someone as beautiful and special for something like her only shows his value, and that he is someone not worth being with you.

"Everyone who seems to be gaining on you are lost and are not secure with themselves, and so like those who start using drugs to impress someone, they are trying to fit in with each other and are only putting you down to make themselves feel good.

"Everyone is trying to be someone else, and they dislike you because you follow your own ambitions and are not doing what others are doing to be the person they want to be.

"Individuality is what separates you. They all are the ones who are losers. People just don't understand you, but it's not for anyone to know or ever understand your ways and why you do the things you do. That is what makes you unique.

"Everybody is always following and doing what everybody else is doing, but that should not be what makes you. It's not about what anyone else thinks about you when you know who you are.

"You must fall in love with who you are and the person you want to be. If you kill yourself by using drugs, or putting a gun to your head to escape, it will only take away the chances of you ever becoming who you could someday possibly become.

"There are more things that matter in life than what people are saying or doing on social media. On social media and the internet, people can be anyone, and anyone can be who they want the lame to believe they are. They are not really liked when they are seen in real life. More than half the people who are friends don't know and have never seen the people they have friended and continue to follow. The friends that people believe they have on social media are not truly friends.

"There are people who have five thousand friends and followers, but they themselves may not have five dollars to feed themselves when they get hungry. If they tell the friends they have on there that they are hungry and need something to eat, out of five thousand how many do you believe will genuinely send them one dollar if he is not a nigga who just wants to fuck?

"Everyone is only feeding the flaws and insecurities of another because of their own weaknesses and need for attention. False attention from likes should never determine the importance of who you are and how you feel about yourself when there are those who get attention by enhancing images and portraying a life they are not truly living.

"If what they are doing is not real and what you see is not who a person is when they portray themselves to the world, then why compare your life and the importance of who you are to a person who is getting attention from a false image? They are not being themselves therefore the attention they get is only an illusion that gives them a false sense of admiration.

"Never give energy to the things that are not real. What you see and are getting from everything that I am giving is what is real. Loving who you are and staying true to what you believe is what life is about. Never give up on yourself for things that don't matter."

Crossing Sunrise Boulevard, driving well below the speed limit, on 27th Avenue past Panther Lane, many of the students had been standing in front the school's entrance near the bus loop.

Noticing Jeremy, who had been with his back against the school's fence while hugging Amelia. Observing Katesha's response as the girl had seemed to follow his eyes, Darrell said, "Are you sure you are going to be good?"

Flashing a light smile as she nodded, Katesha said, "I will be fine, I just hate that I now have to go to school with my hair wild and out like this."

Checking the time on her phone, she said, "And now it's too late for me to go home. If I am tardy then when the school call my auntie, she will want to know why I was late, but honestly this morning when I left it didn't matter because I thought today would be the last day that I would be alive."

Removing the turban from his head as he handed it to the girl, Darrell said, "You can't be seen coming from around me like that, so just tuck all that inside of there."

Reviewing several missed calls and multiple text messages while waiting for the girl to get herself together, Darrell then got out of the SUV and walked around to open the door for her.

Most had never seen him and had only heard rumors about his reputation, though with the many girls who had believed he had been interested in them, never once had any of them ever received any sincere attention.

Watching Jeremy's reaction as the boy now focused more on him than Amelia, she, and everyone else could only stare shocked as Katesha stepped out.

Reaching inside one of the pockets of the black jogging suit as he then flipped through several bills before removing another wad from the other where he peeled loose one thousand dollars.

Hugging the girl as he then kissed her on the forehead, whispering he said, "You don't have to keep it if your auntie Bible teach you not to spend illegal drug money, but when you walk past, look him in the eye and then tell me what do you think he now feels like doing to himself."

According to the National Center for Missing &
Exploited Children, there are thousands of Black
girls who are reported missing each year. There are
families who have lived to see their child return
home, but with many of these children who have
been abducted, molested, and murdered, their cases
were never solved.

2

There is nothing you can expect from anyone if it is not first given to you from yourself. Respect and love from others begin with the love and respect you show yourself.

When many young girls go missing, or their bodies are found in unmarked graves, there is a reason why.

There are cases where some young women are rebellious and have made the decision to run away, but many times when these children leave their homes they are often lured away by a dream of a better life through false promises.

Like most, whose father had been deceased, incarcerated, strung out on drugs, or has neglected his own children to care for those of another woman, Tranice had been raised inside of a single parent home.

When children are raised without the guidance of a true father figure, this often paralyzes and cause them to be subject to the charms of any male who demonstrates the absent affection they have always yearned to receive.

While understanding this behavior many will use it as a tool to exploit their weaknesses.

Angela Harris had worked two jobs to provide for Tranice and her siblings, but still there had been times while her mother struggled to pay bills, she and her sisters had gone hungry and looked forward to the next day when the school would provide breakfast.

The only thing Tranice wanted was a source that would allow her to live a life her mother could not provide. She had heard that she would soon be eligible to apply for a part time position at several fast food restaurants, but while she had seen many girls involved with older men who allowed them to keep up with the latest trends, why should she work anywhere when she could have sex with a "Scammer" or a drug dealer who would pay her twice as much for half the time she would be occupied on a job.

Inspired by female rap artist and television shows that encouraged women to exploit men by taking much more than they themselves should give in return, this was the lifestyle she envisioned.

All she needed to do was meet the right man who would change her life. With the attention she often received Tranice had been very aware of her sex appeal. She had been only weeks away from turning fourteen, but the way her body had developed, she had already possessed many full features that most adult women had gone through intensive surgery to obtain. This she knew was what would also get the attention of those in the industry, and so on the day that she had received a message and a heart on a post from Max, Tranice believed that this had been a calling from God.

Everything about the man's words seemed promising. Not only had she seen pictures of the cars and all the money he made, but he had been friends with a recruiter for a modeling agency, and while his company had been publishing a new magazine that would have her placed on the subscriptions first edition, there had been over a hundred thousand people who followed him on Instagram. He could make her a star and she would have the attention of all those who followed their group.

This exposure would open other doors and with the five thousand dollars he had promised to give to help her pursue a modeling career, those funds would allow her to purchase the latest designer bags and heels. She knew that in exchange Max would want sexual favors, yet to get what she wanted that had been something she was willing to do. It wasn't like she was a virgin, and with all of those she had been with, even though the man had been thirty-six, she believed that she would still be able to handle him.

She had been told by Max to keep both their plans and relationship a secret, and so when she left that morning Tranice had failed to inform Angela or anyone else about where she had been going.

Using the false page he had created disguised as a teenager from another state, after prowling through the friends list of another girl he had targeted, Max had requested to be Tranice's friend and began to study her personality. Each time she expressed her feelings through posts she provided him with more information and the tools he would use to approach her.

This was the advantage of social media. From her profile he discovered that Tranice had aspired to become a model, and this would be the interest he would use to entice her. There were many reasons why he often chose to pursue young black girls. Most were vulnerable due to their family's financial conditions and had any of them ever made any attempts to accuse him of rape, officials would never take them serious and would soon abandon the case.

Behind Marshall's corner store, where he had come that morning after dropping off Katesha, a girl who had been contemplating suicide and planned to murder her boyfriend, Darrell observed the driver of a white Lexus LC500 coupe.

With the constant flow of drug traffic, it had been common for whites to frequent the area, although at the time the headlights on the vehicle began to glare, Darrell noticed Tranice making her way stealthily toward the Lexus.

Tranice who had once lived directly across the street from him had been the niece of an older man he had once admired, though what had been less about who the girl had been related to, while aware of what had been transpiring, he refused to allow her to leave with him.

It had been disturbing to think of any white man having sex with a black woman. That had been the worst thing that any black woman could do. For years he had witnessed how many white men had preyed upon young black women, and how often they were easily deceived and manipulated. It had been a sad thing to see how lost and blind many of them were.

Exiting the SUV as he walked over and stood in front of the Lexus so the man could not drive away. Approaching the driver's side as he spoke to the girl, Darrell said, "What does this suppose to be? You are not going anywhere with this cracker."

Studying the school uniform the girl had been wearing, whereas even though he acknowledged how thick she had grown to be, there had been nothing to take away the youth that was clearly visible in her facial features.

He had known many older men who often had sex with underage girls claim they could not tell or did not know that most had been the age they were, but while looking in Tranice's face, even with her being only three years younger, he recognized an innocence that caused him to determine that she had even been too young for him.

Observing the girl's reaction being that after he had signaled for her to back away from the car, Darrell had drawn a gun and punched the man in the face.

Confused and undecided of whether she should walk away as he then called her over to him, Darrell said, "Check this out."

Aware of the boy's reputation, being that she had heard rumors of the cruel things he had done to people, though while he had never been opposed and seen as a threat to her, as he now spoke, his expression and the fierceness of his words made her unsure if whether he would hit her the same way he had done Max.

Looking around at several bystanders who were watching and possibly wondering what had caused the Lexus to speed away as he now spoke low in a subdued tone, Darrell said, "I know it is not my place to try to control your life and tell you what to do, but when I see you and think about all the other little girls that are lost and being misguided this is something that I have to give you.

"You have fuck niggas and slick ass crackers all around the world who manipulate and take advantage of the minds of little girls. It is not a color thing. When some look at most they will never expect them to become a victim. These are the ones who a lot of times come up missing or are found dead. There is a possibility that some of these men are just looking for one of you to have sex, but still what if that same man decided that he didn't want to pay you or that he wanted to have sex without a condom?

"How would you stop him? He could have got you to his house or a hotel and drugged you, and while you are alone and helpless, he could do whatever he wants to you. There are a lot of men who are carrying HIV and with most of those who have AIDS that is how they spread it. They find little girls who are easy to manipulate and give them that shit. Just because a man looks like he has money doesn't mean that he is healthy. Don't ever degrade your worth as a queen by selling your body for materialistic things that don't matter. A man is not the only way you could make it or provide for yourself in life. No matter what anybody promises you, you can't never trust and go anywhere with anyone you don't really know. As a queen, and a black goddess of this world, every time we lose one of you a part of us is taken away."

How many men will see a 12-year-old having sex or selling her body and pull her aside to redirect her? To do that a lot of men will see it as flaw. When a female is conscious, she can no longer be taken advantage of. With many being so lost, you will have some of those same girls that you try to save despise you and would prefer to have sex for money rather than listen to your advice. Whether any female appears unreceptive or too far gone in the streets it is our duty to empower our women. There are many men who will get together and have sex with a twelve-year-old like she is an animal, and then sell her to another group of men for them to have repeated sex. When there is a man who is only thinking about the feeling he gets from ejaculation, and not the future of what this little girl could become he will try to manipulate and have sex with her before he tries to open her eyes. You say that you are a real man, but what is real in that? I'm a real man and to me that is not what real men do. Any man who can only think with the idea of the pleasures that he will receive from sex is weak and will never be in control of himself. This is where most men fall short of glory. When we disrespect and take advantage of our young women, they then grow to believe that such a way is the way a woman should be treated, and that is why she allows herself, and her body to be disrespected. Our women are a reflection of our creation, and so for that which we install, these are the traits that will be reflected through their representation.

The same reason that most men approach women only to have sex, when a woman takes her clothes off and have sex easily, she does that when she doesn't have nothing more in her head. Sex is the only way she can communicate. With her being mis-led without guidance she doesn't know any other way to impress a man, so she opens her legs and have sex freely without thinking about the love she needs to have for herself before she can get anyone else to love her. Don't ever forget that you are a queen and a goddess of the universe. Even if you are really attracted to any man the way you have never been with any other before don't ever compromise your morals because you want that man to want you. You will end up with the type of man that you allow in your life. When you settle for a man who is incapable of contributing to that which you expect and deserve as a woman that is what you will get. Every man that you like is not always the right one for you, and that is what you need to be looking for, a man that is right for you. There will come a lot of times that you may feel lonely, but still, you don't ever chase a man. If you ever want to be respected, you first must love yourself and focus on who you want to be. The best thing that any man can have, is a woman that has her head on right, but yet while most men are green, they do not look for a woman that is living right and has something to think with. Most men are looking for the easy woman who is willing to have sex the moment they meet. When he meets a woman who lives by a moral code that guides her conduct the objective is to break her down, so with that, don't ever allow a man to bring you to disgrace by lowering your value and worth as a woman.

There are some I may never meet, but to you who have read and received the message that I intend to deliver, understand that there is something special about you. There is something in you and I believe that you have the potential to be something more than you may see right now. This message that I am delivering was never intended to control your life, but still while you are living your life and doing the things that you are doing, I want you to use your mind dand be a thinker for me. There are many young women who were never blessed with the privilege of having someone guide them. By the age of fourteen they were already pregnant and may now have three or four children by someone who may only be known to them by a nickname. No matter what some may believe or how real of a man any man may be considered, the truth is that a woman like that appears worthless to someone who has plans and is going anywhere. I know what you can become if you apply these lessons and play your cards right. You are only considered and will be recognized as a real woman, and a queen when you apply those principles and conduct yourself in such manner. There is nothing wrong with living your life and doing things that bring you happiness but understanding that certain moments that many get caught up in weren't designed to be forever. Don't get caught up with any man who doesn't have any real plans for himself and his future and allow him to trick and take away your value. No matter how much you like him or how good the things that he is doing make you feel, always make him use a condom. The results that we receive in life are determined by our choices, and every choice that you make will determine where and how you are perceived when it will matter the most.

About the Author

Darrell Dwayne Bernard Mallard II, is a writer dedicated to confronting the challenges of society and life by sharing these truths with readers who he aspires to reach and give direction through insight and enlightenment. Born in Fort Lauderdale, Florida, Darrell relates these stories to those that reflect his own experiences and the struggle of others.

Printed in the USA
CPSIA information can be obtained
at www.ICGtesting.com
LVHW090640131024
793633LV00001B/158